WALT DISNEY'S CLASSIC

Based on Walt Disney Pictures'
Featurette

Adapted by Nancy E. Krulik

SCHOLASTIC INC.
New York Toronto London Auckland Sydney

ISBN 0-590-44364-X

12 11 10 9 8 7 6 5 4 3 2 1 0 1 2 3 4 5/9

Printed in the U.S.A. 40

First Scholastic printing, November 1990

Introduction

A long, long time ago, England was ruled by a fair and wise King. The people lived happily. They had plenty of juicy turkey, tangy cranberries, hot tea, and sweet biscuits to fill their stomachs. They had soft beds to sleep in, and thick shoes and wool overcoats to keep them warm and dry during the cold, wet English winters.

But by and by, the good King grew too old and sick to rule his kingdom.

The greedy Captain of the Guards saw the King's weakness as a chance to make himself rich. The Captain and his group of guards traveled through the land and stole from the people — until the people had nothing left for them to steal!

As if that weren't bad enough, the Captain of the Guards told everyone he was stealing by order of the King. Of course the poor old King really knew nothing of the Captain's cruel deeds or just how poor his people had become because of them.

It seemed that no one could save the kingdom from the evil Captain of the Guards until one very special day, when the King's son met a poor beggar boy. . . .

1

"Kindling! Fresh kindling!" Mickey called from his place on the busy London street corner. Mickey was trying to sell firewood to the people as they rushed home for the night. Mickey was a poor fellow. Selling wood on the street was the way he made money for dinner. Mickey spoke with a hopeful voice as people passed him.

"You can't cook dinner without a fire can you, sir?" he called after one man. But the man just pulled his scarf tighter around his neck and kept walking. He didn't even look at the little pauper.

"Sir . . ." Mickey called again. But the man was long gone. *Well, he can't*, Mickey thought to himself. Mickey shrugged and pulled his ragged coat around him. It barely kept him warm. The holes in the wool let all the cold air in. The little pauper yanked his floppy green wool hat down over his chilled ears. He shuddered slightly as the cold wind whooshed around his head.

Mickey's stomach growled with hunger. He hadn't eaten a thing all day. But Mickey ignored his hungry belly. There was work to be done! He called out cheerfully to another customer.

"Kindling! Kindling! Anyone need any kindling?" No one stopped to buy. Still, Mickey didn't get sad. He always believed good luck was waiting just around the corner.

Mickey heard barking, and up bounded his faithful pup, Pluto. The dog snuggled his brown furry body against his master's leg for warmth. Pluto looked up hopefully at Mickey. Then he dropped his long pink tongue out of his mouth. A drop of water fell from his lips.

"I know, fella. I'm hungry, too." Mickey comforted him. He petted Pluto lovingly.

The dog looked up at Mickey with sad eyes. Slowly he wagged his tail, and licked Mickey's face. No matter how cold or hungry Pluto was, Mickey always made him feel better just by being there.

"Hiya, Goofy, how's business?" Mickey called to his pal.

Goofy was standing a few feet from Mickey, trying to sell snow cones. "Snow cones!" he called. "We've got plain, and rock, and twig." But the weather was cold and wet. The people passing by did not buy snow cones. They wanted hot tea with their dinner.

"Gawrsh, Mickey," Goofy sighed, "if I don't get a customer soon, I may have to eat these snow cones myself."

Mickey looked at Goofy and Pluto. His two closest friends sure looked unhappy. Mickey knew he had to cheer them up.

"Aw, don't look so sad, guys," he smiled bravely. Pluto and Goofy didn't return his smile. They looked sadly at the ground instead.

So Mickey spread his smile even wider. "Come on, fellas, secret handshake!" He held out his hand.

Goofy looked at his unsold snow cones. Then he looked at Mickey. "Humm . . . okay!" he said and smiled. He put his hand against Mickey's.

Pluto placed his paw on top of Goofy's hand. The threesome lowered their hands to the ground, then raised them high in the air. They laughingly wiggled their fingers in a secret handshake of friendship and support.

Mickey pointed to a tall stone castle on a far-off hill. It could be seen over the thatched roofs of the cottages and tiny shops that lined the city streets. The King and his family lived in the castle. They almost never came down from their castle to visit the town. They never saw how poor the people had become.

"One of these days we'll be doing everything like the royal family," Mickey laughed. "We'll be eating just like them."

Then he started to sing a song about what it would be like to be a king. He sang about how he would eat turkey, potatoes, rolls, corn, even a pizza pie.

Mickey laughed as he tossed a pizza made of snow in the air, just like a pizza-maker in a pizza shop would do.

Pluto ran around at Mickey's feet and took a big bite of the snow pizza!

Goofy started to play the game, too. He took some snow and sculpted a tasty suckling pig with an apple in its mouth. He rubbed his skinny belly. "Just to make my belly fat," he said with a giggle.

Mickey pulled even harder on his thin woolen cap as he thought about what it would be like to be a king. He could really use a warm hat to wear.

Goofy thought long red thermal underwear would be nice — especially the old-fashioned kind with the flap in the back.

The idea of being warm and cozy with full stomachs made the two friends so happy that they did a silly jig right there in the middle of the street! Pluto wagged his tail wildly. He barked in agreement.

Before long, the three of them were singing, dancing, and laughing so hard that they forgot how hungry they felt. They didn't even realize that it had begun to snow.

But Mickey, Goofy, and Pluto's fun was short-lived. Soon their happy voices were drowned out by the loud *clip-clop clip-clop clip-clop* of the royal horses. The horses pulled the royal coach through the cobblestone streets. The coach carried a band of evil weasel guards.

The weasels were in a jolly mood. They had just come from stealing the last bit of food from the orphanage! Stealing from the poor was their favorite thing to do. Of course the weasel guards did all of their mischief under orders from their boss — the wicked Captain Pete!

The weasels' cackling voices rang through the streets as the coach carried them back home to the castle. As they rode along they sang about Captain Pete and his wicked deeds. The weasels laughed hysterically with their shrill shrieking voices.

Mickey and Goofy ran and hid in a dark alleyway as the weasels rode by. They were afraid of the mean, long-necked, pointy-nosed creatures. Everyone knew the weasels beat up on poor, innocent folks — just for fun.

But Pluto wasn't afraid of the weasels at all. He was just mad that they had spoiled his good time with Mickey and Goofy! With a loud, angry bark, Pluto darted out into the street and took off after the carriage. He ran alongside the coach, jumping up and down. He howled at the weasels.

Mickey stared at his dog in horror! Had Pluto gone completely crazy? Mickey had to stop him! Quickly Mickey ran out into the street. He tried to catch up with his dog. "Pluto! Pluto! No!" Mickey called out as he ran.

But Mickey's two tiny feet were no match for Pluto's four quick-moving paws. Before he could catch Pluto, Mickey watched him follow the carriage up the big hill. Pluto ran right through the castle gates!

2

The huge wooden castle gates slammed shut in Mickey's face! Now Pluto was on the inside, and Mickey was stuck on the outside.

"Pluto! Pluto!" Mickey called out. "Pluto!" But Pluto didn't answer.

Mickey folded his hands into tight little fists. He banged on the heavy gates.

"Who goes there and what do you want?" a loud, deep voice asked from inside the gates.

Mickey jumped up and tried to see who was talking. The voice was coming from the gatekeeper. It was the gatekeeper's job to make sure no unwelcome guests got into the castle. Mickey knew he and Pluto were probably unwelcome guests.

"Um, gosh," Mickey answered nervously. "I . . . I just want to get my dog back. He ran in before I could catch him."

The gatekeeper peered through a window in the wooden gate. He took one look at Mickey and snapped to attention.

"Y-Y-Your Majesty," he stuttered as he unlocked the gates. "I, uh, d-d-do come in, sire. Forgive me . . . will you ever forgive me? Beautiful day, isn't it?" The gatekeeper bowed low to the ground.

Mickey rushed past the gatekeeper. "Gee, thanks," he called to the fellow as he ran off in search of Pluto. Then he realized that the gatekeeper had called him "sire." Mickey was puzzled, but he didn't have time to go back and ask any questions. He had to find Pluto.

As he was running, Mickey felt a strong hand grab the back of his coat. The huge, hairy hand lifted him off the ground.

"Hey! What's the idea . . ." Mickey started to shout. Mickey swung around. He looked straight into the meanest, ugliest, cigar-chomping face he had ever seen. It was Captain Pete, Captain of the Guards!

Captain Pete held Mickey in midair. In his other hand he held poor Pluto by the tail. Captain Pete dragged the two of them back to the castle gates.

When Pete reached the gates, the gatekeeper was still bowing.

"What do you think this is," Captain Pete barked at the gatekeeper, "open house?"

The gatekeeper looked up from the ground to see Pete's shiny black boots. He straightened ever so slowly and looked innocently at Captain Pete.

"B-But Captain, th-th-that was the Prince," he explained.

Captain Pete lifted up one of his sharp boots. Wham! He stamped it down hard on the gatekeeper's foot.

"Oh, yeah? Then who's that, numbskull?" Pete snarled, pointing over at a castle window.

The gatekeeper gulped. There wasn't much else he could do. Mickey couldn't possibly be the Prince! The gatekeeper could see the Prince through the window clear as day.

3

The Prince sat in the castle classroom with his servant, Donald, and his teacher, Sir Horace. Sir Horace was giving the Prince his evening lesson.

The Prince hated listening to Horace's lectures. He didn't want to be cooped up in a tiny little room learning about the ancient Greek alphabet. He wanted to be outside laughing and playing in the snow.

The Prince looked longingly out the window. From his seat he could see a group of poor London children building a snowman on the side of a hill. That's where the Prince wanted to be right now.

"Sire!" Horace broke into the Prince's daydream. "Sire, you really must give me your full attention. Now we shall discuss ancient Greek writings."

Horace droned on and on. Instead of taking notes, the Prince took a peashooter out of his pocket. Carefully he loaded it with a tiny pea.

Ptooie! The pea flew out of the shooter. It hit Donald Duck in the back of the neck.

"Waak!" Donald cried. "What the heck was that?"

The Prince looked innocently at Donald. Then he smiled at Horace. "Do go on, Horace," he said.

Horace continued his speech. Once again, the Prince loaded his peashooter and blew.

Ptooie! The pea soared across the room. It bounced off Donald's back.

"Wak!" Donald squawked again, rubbing his sore back.

Horace ignored Donald and kept on talking. The Prince grinned and loaded his shooter with a third pea. This one landed right on the white tail feathers that covered Donald's behind.

Bull's-eye! the Prince thought to himself.

Finally, Donald figured out what the Prince was up to. *Well, two can play at this game,* Donald thought to himself. He loaded his peashooter. Donald placed the shooter to his bill and blew. The pea flew across the room, landing squarely . . . against Horace's behind!

"Ouch!" Horace shouted. He turned angrily to Donald and put one hand on his hip. "Now, Donald," he said, "I'll have you know I do not find your behavior — "

"But he started it," Donald said, pointing angrily at the Prince.

But Horace didn't want to hear it. He started scolding Donald.

Donald had to try hard not to laugh while Horace talked. The Prince was standing behind Horace, imitating everything the old teacher did. Horace wagged his finger at Donald. The Prince wagged his finger. Horace folded his arms against his chest. The Prince folded his arms. Horace leaned back and looked angrily at Donald. The Prince leaned back and looked angrily at Donald, too.

Finally, Donald burst out laughing so hard at the Prince's joke that he fell flat on the floor!

"Donald! That's it! Get out!" Horace ordered.

Donald put his head down and walked out the door. "Ah, phooey," he mumbled angrily. "I always get in trouble because of that stupid prince!"

As Donald left, Horace scolded the Prince. "And as for you, Your Highness," he said, "you know your father is ill and requires rest and quiet. Now, sire, if we may continue with . . ."

Pluto's loud barking in the courtyard drowned out the rest of Horace's speech. The Prince ran to the window to find out what was going on.

"Beat it . . . ya dumb mutt," Captain Pete shouted at Pluto. The Captain was holding Mickey in one hand while shaking his own leg high in the air. Pluto was holding onto Captain Pete's leg with his teeth. "Get out of here! Let go of my leg," he shouted at Pluto.

"Captain! I say, Captain," the Prince called down. "What's the meaning of this uproar?"

At the sound of the Prince's voice, Captain Pete snapped to attention. And that was no easy task. After all, he had a squirming pauper in his left hand and a big brown dog attached to his right leg!

"Just some, ah, local riffraff," the Captain answered.

"Even the lowliest subjects of this kingdom deserve some respect," the Prince said. "Unhand that lad immediately!"

Kerplunk! Captain Pete dropped Mickey to the ground.

"Now apologize to him," the Prince ordered.

Captain Pete growled under his breath. He really hated saying he was sorry.

"Uh, one of these days . . . I'm going to . . . sorry, punk!" he muttered to Mickey.

"Now have him brought to me at once," the Prince continued.

Captain Pete snarled. "The Prince wishes to see you," he smiled. "Allow me!" Then he kicked Mickey into a huge pile of snow. He laughed while he watched Mickey dig himself out.

Pluto gazed at his master and whimpered. Pluto wanted to visit the Prince, too.

"Stay, Pluto. I'll be right back!" Mickey called to his dog.

Pluto looked angrily at Captain Pete and snarled.

"Grrrrrrrrr!!" Pete growled back. He picked Pluto up and kicked him like a football! Pluto flew over the castle gates. He landed in a pile of snow in the street. Now Mickey was on the inside, and Pluto was on the outside.

Captain Pete laughed as he walked off toward the castle.

4

Mickey couldn't believe his eyes. He'd never been inside a castle. It was the most beautiful place he had ever seen. The walls were covered with brightly colored paintings of famous English battles. Glistening crystal chandeliers hung low in the hallways. The window drapes were made of velvet. The mirrors were framed in real gold.

In front of each mirror was a suit of armor. Each suit was set at attention, as if it were going to fight any minute!

Mickey looked down at the black-and-white marble floors. They were so shiny that he could see himself.

"Wow! Huh! Hiya!" Mickey waved to his reflection. Mickey was very excited about being in the castle. He started to dance a happy jig and sing his song about being a king.

Suddenly Mickey crashed into an empty suit of armor. "Excuse me," he said to the armor.

The suit of armor teeter-tottered back and forth.

"Whoa! Steady, fella," Mickey said. He tried to hold the armor up. But Mickey was too small to keep the heavy suit of armor from collapsing. The helmet fell off. It landed right on Mickey's head! Then, one by one, all the suits of armor went crashing to the floor like dominoes!

The Prince ran into the hallway. "What in the world is going on out here?!" the Prince yelled over the loud noise. Before he could get an answer, a metal helmet landed on his head.

"Huh?" said the Prince.

"Who turned out the lights?" Mickey asked nervously. He took a step forward in the dark.

"Donald," the Prince accused as he

walked slowly. "If this is your idea of a joke, I'm going to . . ."

Clunk! Mickey and the Prince smacked right into each other.

Slowly, Mickey and the Prince lifted the visors on their helmets.

"Aaaah!" Mickey screamed. "You look just like . . ."

"Aaaah!" the Prince screamed. "You look just like . . ."

"I thought you were . . ." Mickey gasped.

"I thought you were . . ." the Prince gasped at the same time.

Mickey and the Prince couldn't believe their eyes. They looked exactly alike!

5

The Prince took a second to catch his breath. Seeing someone who looked just like himself was quite a shock!

"Wait, wait, wait. Now just a second. Who are you?" the Prince asked Mickey. "And who is your tailor?" he added, after he looked at Mickey's ragged clothes.

"Ah . . . ah . . . the name's Mickey, Your . . . Your Royal Highness . . ."

"Ah, the beggar boy," the Prince smiled knowingly. "Well, Mickey, I must thank you for saving my life."

Mickey's eyes opened wide. "Saving your life?" he asked.

The Prince giggled. "I was about to die

of boredom when you interrupted my lesson. Do you know what it is like to be the Prince?" he sighed.

Mickey's eyes opened even wider. "Oh, boy! It must be fun."

The Prince shook his head. "Never a moment to myself. Breakfast at seven."

Mickey rubbed his hungry stomach. "Breakfast," he muttered.

"Lessons 'til lunch," the Prince continued.

"Lunch!" Mickey licked his lips.

"Fencing 'til teatime! And every night, banquet after feast after banquet," the Prince added.

All that food sounded perfect to Mickey. "Wow!" was all he could say.

"And then nine o'clock — bedtime."

"Beddy-bye," Mickey smiled dreamily.

"And that's every day," the Prince explained.

"Wow! Every day!" Mickey said.

The Prince sighed. "How I envy you and your freedom," he said to Mickey. "Games all day long. No studying dreary old books. Staying up as late as you like. Eating junk food. Oh, if I could take your place for just one day . . ." The Prince stopped in midsentence. He had a wonderful idea!

The Prince took off his velvet hat and handed it to Mickey. Then he grabbed Mickey's floppy hat and put it on his own head. The two of them looked in the mirror.

"Don't you see," the Prince said, grinning. "I shall take your place with your friends in the streets of London, and you shall be the Prince."

Mickey looked in the mirror. This didn't sound so great to him. "Th-Th-The Prince? Huh! I can't be the Prince," Mickey gasped. "H-H-How would I act?"

The Prince looked Mickey straight in the eye. "You needn't worry, lad. To rule, you need say one of two things. 'That's a splendid idea, I'm glad I thought of it!' and 'Guards, seize him!' "

Mickey repeated after the Prince. *That isn't so hard*, he thought.

"Well, come on, then," the Prince said.

He took off his red velvet robe and handed it to Mickey.

In no time at all, Mickey found himself dressed in the Prince's soft satin suit and velvet robes. He looked in the mirror and stroked the purple feather that stood straight up from the Prince's hat. Mickey had never worn such fine clothes.

The Prince stood next to Mickey. He looked in the mirror and admired his new rags. "No one will know I'm not you and you are not me," the Prince declared.

"B-B-But your father, the King!" Mickey said nervously.

The Prince placed his hand on Mickey's shoulder. "I'll be back in the wink of an eye! And if there's any trouble, all may know me by this." The Prince flashed a ring under Mickey's nose.

Mickey stared at the ring. It had the royal crest on it and was covered with jewels. Mickey had never seen a royal ring in his life. It was so big and bright!

"Wow!" he exclaimed. "But I'm still not sure this is a good idea. I . . ."

"You'll do fine, Mickey," the Prince assured him. "You're looking more royal already."

Before Mickey could say another word, the Prince hoisted himself up on the window ledge. Carefully, he held onto the ivy vines that lined the outer walls of the castle. The Prince slowly lowered himself to the ground.

"Well, uh, you won't forget to come back, will you?" Mickey laughed nervously after him. "G'bye," he added in a very small voice.

6

The Prince skipped happily onto the palace lawn. He wasn't wasting any time. This was his first day as a regular, everyday, run-of-the-mill peasant.

But as he got closer to the gate, the Prince became nervous. What if he didn't look as much like a commoner as he thought? What if someone recognized him?

Captain Pete was standing guard at the gate. He took one look at the Prince and smiled an evil grin. He was sure that the Prince was Mickey Mouse. Captain Pete lit his cigar. He blew a huge puff of smoke — right into the Prince's face!

The Prince choked on the smelly brown smoke.

"Ah, my little peasant. Embarrass me in

front of the Prince, will you!" Captain Pete bellowed. He blew an even bigger cloud of smoke into the Prince's face.

The Prince coughed — but this time with a smile on his face. He had fooled Captain Pete!

"Peasant?" the Prince said with a laugh, then coughed again. "Captain, I've fooled you. I am the Prince!"

Captain Pete looked at the little green floppy hat and the ragged wool coat the Prince was wearing. He started to laugh. "Oh! Forgive me, Your Highness. Allow me," he said with a cruel chuckle. Captain Pete took the Prince by the arm and helped him into a basket-shaped chair.

"How thoughtful of you, Captain," the Prince said.

Captain Pete snickered. "I live to serve," he sneered. Then he yanked on a thick rope that was attached to the chair. Suddenly the chair rose high over the palace gates. Captain Pete gave the rope one more tug and the Prince flew out of the chair — way over the gates! The Prince landed in a pile of snow on the street.

"So long, sucker." Captain Pete laughed as he chewed on his cigar. He puffed out his huge chest and walked back toward the castle.

Outside, the Prince dug himself out of the snow and looked around. "Pfft." He spit some snow out of his mouth. *I fooled him!* the Prince thought to himself. *Oh, I'm good! I can fool anyone!*

But the Prince was wrong. He couldn't fool everyone into thinking he was Mickey. Before the Prince knew what was happening, Pluto ran over and pounced on him.

At first, even Pluto was fooled by the Prince's disguise. But after a few sniffs and licks, the puppy jumped away from the Prince. Pluto sadly walked away. He knew this imposter wasn't Mickey at all!

The Prince watched as Pluto trudged down the street alone. "Well, for now, nothing's going to spoil my fun," the Prince said with a determined look on his face.

Before the Prince could take a single step toward the center of the city, a huge, long-eared fellow with big buck teeth and a guffawing laugh rushed up and hugged him!

"Hey, Mickey! There you are!" Goofy cried affectionately. He squeezed the Prince even tighter.

The Prince mumbled from between Goofy's arms.

"Where'd you go, Mickey?" Goofy asked. "Come here, you little nut," he laughed.

Goofy was so excited to see his pal Mickey. The silly guy took the Prince's head under his arm and playfully dug his fist in between the Prince's ears. "Noogy, noogy, noogy!" Goofy laughed. Then he let go of the Prince's head and raised his right hand.

"C'mon, gimme that secret handshake, Mick! C'mon, put your hand down there! C'mon, swing it up here! C'mon a-boola, boola, boola, boola!"

The Prince looked oddly at Goofy. Secret handshake? The Prince had never heard of any secret handshake.

"C'mon, Mickey," Goofy said again.

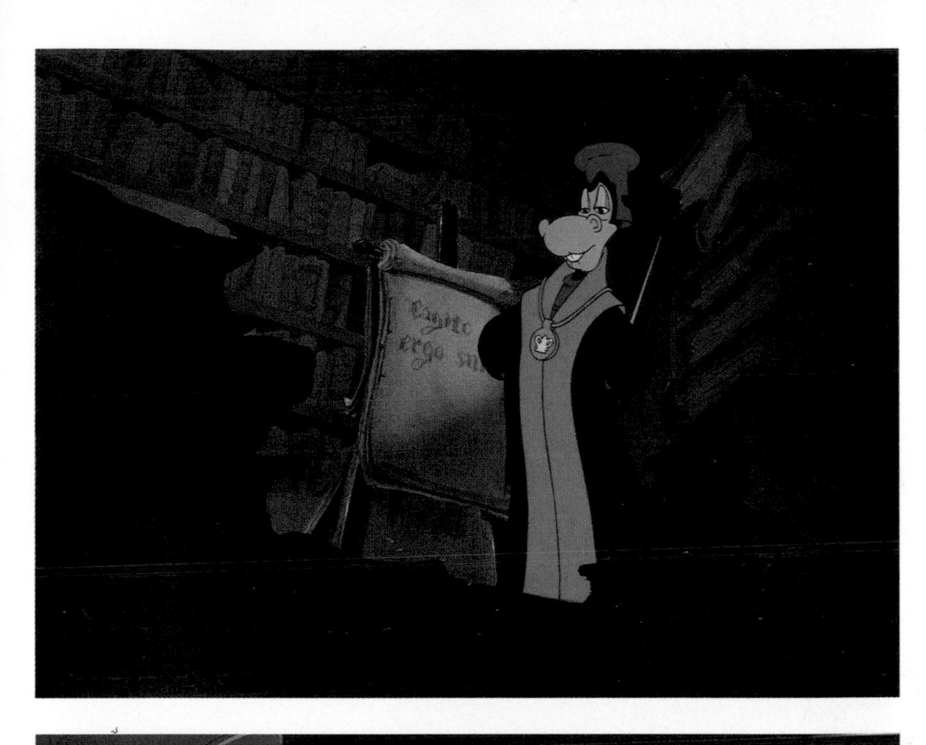
ergo

"Oh, yes, that is me, Mickey Mouse. Peasant at large," the Prince said remembering. He was also trying very hard to sound like a poor peasant. He sounded like a prince anyway.

"You must forgive me," the Prince continued, "but I am dreadful with names. Um, could I have your name?"

"What's the matter with the one you got? Hyuck. I'm Goofy, remember?"

The Prince nodded. "So I see," he said with concern. "My dear man, if there is anything I can do to help, by all means, let me know."

Goofy laughed hard and smacked the Prince on the back. "Hyuck! Hyuck! I get it. It's a joke! That's a good one, Mick."

The Prince was anxious to get into the center of the city. He pretended to look down at his watch. "Will you look at the time?" he said quickly to Goofy. "I really must be going." Then, with a very royal wave of his handkerchief, the Prince was off — ready to live one day as the beggar boy, Mickey!

7

The real Mickey was back at the castle, having a lesson with Horace about foreign countries.

But Mickey wasn't listening to a word old Horace was saying. He was too hungry to pay attention. Instead, Mickey was dreaming about food — sausages, pancakes, potato salad, chocolate bunnies. . . .

Mickey's delicious daydreams were cut short by a loud noise. Donald burst through the door with the Prince's dinner cart.

"La, la, la," Donald sang. "Suppertime, my lord!"

"Oh, boy! Food!" Mickey exclaimed.

Mickey's stomach growled. He watched

hungrily as Donald carved some juicy white meat from a turkey breast.

"We have time for only one more question, Highness," Horace was saying. "Now . . . Constantinople is the capital of what country?"

Mickey stared as Donald added vegetables and stuffing to the turkey platter.

"Turkey . . ." he said, drooling.

Horace smiled. "Turkey is correct. Until next time . . ."

Before Horace could get out the door, Mickey took a flying leap across the room toward the food. He grabbed an apple and opened his mouth.

Donald knocked the apple out of Mickey's hand. "Wak! Stop!" he warned. "I have to taste it first!"

Mickey stared at Donald. Then he remembered he was supposed to be a prince. "Uh, that's a splendid idea. I'm glad I thought of it." Mickey smiled proudly. He sounded just like the real Prince.

Donald breathed in the sweet smell of the

turkey. With a chuckle he bit into a piece of tasty turkey with giblet gravy.

"Could be dangerous," he explained between bites of roasted turkey.

Mickey stared as Donald tasted a huge spoonful of stuffing.

"No, that's not poison," Donald said, reaching for a roll, "but let's try . . ."

Desperately, Mickey reached for a turkey leg. Donald kept it away from him.

"No, no, no," Donald scolded. Then he smacked his lips. "Oh, boy, this is good stuff."

Finally Mickey had had enough. After all, he was the Prince.

"I . . . uh . . . I . . . hereby decree that I don't need my food tasted anymore!" Mickey announced in his most princely voice.

"What!" Donald shouted. "Oh, no, you don't!"

Mickey grabbed the turkey leg out of Donald's hand. "I insist! Now hand it over!"

Donald grabbed the leg back. "I'm the royal valet, and I'll tell you when you can eat. Get away from me! Get away from me!"

Donald took the turkey leg and ran! Mickey was right behind him.

"Come back here!" Mickey screamed. "*I'm the Prince!*"

"Ahhh . . ." Donald said as he headed for the door.

Mickey grabbed the turkey leg as Donald went by. He booted Donald out the door, then slammed it in Donald's face!

"Thanks for lunch!" Mickey laughed triumphantly from his side of the door.

Donald pounded angrily on the door for a while. Finally he gave up. "There's something funny about that boy," Donald said.

8

The Prince looked at his reflection in the pastry shop window. He almost did not recognize himself! With the clothes he had on, he looked just like Mickey!

The wind began to blow. The Prince pulled Mickey's coat closer to him. It was very cold out. Back in the castle there would be a warm fire burning and hot tea to drink, *Still*, the Prince thought cheerfully, *I am free and ready for any excitement that might come my way.*

"My turn! My turn!"

The Prince looked away from the shop window to see three children snapping icicles off a store awning. The Prince wanted to play, too. He yanked at an icicle that hung from the awning. It was stuck hard. The

Prince tugged and tugged at the icicle until he yanked it free.

Before the Prince could move out of the way, a huge pile of snow fell off the awning! It covered the Prince. He looked like a giant snowball.

The children laughed. "Good one, mister!"

The Prince stood up. He took off his green cap and bowed to the kids. *I'm glad I made them laugh*, the Prince thought.

Back at the castle courtyard, Mickey was having his first lesson in the art of falconry.

"Now, before you can teach your falcon to hunt, sire," Horace explained, "he must become used to being around you."

Mickey followed all of Horace's instructions exactly. He removed the leather hood from the bird's head. Then he sent him out to hunt. The bird spread his mighty black wings and took a short flight around the yard. Then, instead of chasing a wild animal, he started chasing Mickey around the courtyard.

"Hey! Watch it! That was close!" Mickey shouted as the bird flew over his head!

The Prince wasn't having much better luck out in the street. He felt very lonely. He desperately wanted someone to play with.

The Prince smiled when he saw a stray dog wandering through the narrow streets. The dog was carrying a large bone in his mouth. The Prince wanted to play fetch, so he grabbed the bone out of the mutt's jaws and threw it down an alleyway.

Instead of chasing after the bone, the angry dog took off after the Prince! Before the Prince knew it, a whole gang of street dogs was chasing after him. The poor Prince finally had to leap over a wooden fence to get away from the angry pack.

That was close, the Prince thought as he wiped some sweat from his forehead.

The Prince didn't have time to rest up from his run. There was a fight in the street in front of him. The Prince didn't know it yet, but he was about to be called on to help.

9

"Hey! Leave my mom alone!"

The Prince watched curiously as some street children had an argument with a pack of palace weasel guards.

"You're gonna get it for this," one of the children cried out. "Leave her alone!"

One weasel guard gave the youngsters a dirty look. With a sneer he grabbed the chicken their mother was carrying.

"Somebody help me!" the woman cried out to the crowd.

"Relax, lady," the weasel whined. "It's for the King."

"Yeah, the King," the other weasels laughed.

"But it's all we have," the poor peasant woman pleaded.

"Then it's all we'll take!"

The Prince got so angry that he forgot he was supposed to be Mickey! He stood up and said in a very royal tone, "Halt! As your royal Prince, I command you to unhand that hen!"

The palace guards took one look at the raggedy little pauper in his tattered coat and threadbare hat and started to laugh.

"What is so amusing?" the Prince asked.

One of the guards bowed very low. He picked up a big orange pumpkin. "Forgive me," he said. "I think you forgot your . . . crown!" With that he smashed the pumpkin onto the Prince's head.

The Prince spit a pumpkin seed at the guards as they ran off with the chicken. "When I get back to the palace, you'll pay for this," he said angrily.

A few of the children went to the Prince and helped him to his feet.

"Hey, are you okay?" one asked him.

"I can't believe it," the Prince said, dazed. "Stealing in the King's name."

"It happens all the time," the oldest child explained.

"Yeah, the King takes all our food," said another child.

"And I'm hungry," said the smallest.

The oldest child said something else, but the Prince couldn't hear him. All he could hear was the *clip-clop clip-clop* of horses' hooves. The Royal Provisioner's wagon was coming down the road.

Before the old King became ill, the Royal Provisioner gave food to the needy. But these days, the Royal Provisioner used his wagon to cart the food the weasels had stolen. He brought it all back to Captain Pete.

"Out of the way, you slugs," the driver ordered.

The Prince looked down at his royal ring. He knew he would have to forget about being just another citizen. Right now, the people needed him to be the Prince.

The Prince stood in the wagon's path.

"Halt!" he ordered. "I am the Prince, and I command you to surrender all the food in this wagon."

The driver looked at the Prince. "And I'm the Queen Mother," he said mockingly. "Be off with you!"

The Prince reached up. He shoved the royal ring under the driver's nose.

"Will this help?" he asked.

The driver gasped when he saw the royal crest. A murmur ran through the crowd. "It *is* the Prince! It is the Prince. He has the royal ring!"

The driver stepped aside immediately. He opened the back of the wagon for the Prince.

The Prince handed a chicken to the poor peasant woman who had just been robbed by the weasels. "For you, madam," the Prince said kindly.

"Oh, thank you, sire!" the woman said with a curtsy.

Goofy suddenly joined the crowd. He had been out searching for his pal, Mickey. Imagine how surprised he was to see someone he thought was Mickey, handing out food from the Royal Provisioner's wagon!

Gawrsh, Mickey's flipped his wig! Goofy thought.

He watched the Prince throw a ham into the crowd. "From His Majesty, the King," the Prince said.

A man caught the ham. "Thank you, sire," he said before walking down the street toward his cottage.

"Hey, Mickey!" Goofy shouted. "You're going to get into trouble, doggone it." Then he took off after the man who had caught the ham.

Down the street, the weasels were taking candy from a baby when they heard the shouting. Immediately they ran over to the crowd. They held out their swords and began slicing a path through the mob.

"All right . . . All right . . . Clear out! Out of the way before I bop you," one guard cried.

The driver of the Royal Provisioner's

wagon pointed to the Prince. "He's the one who showed me the ring, sir!" he told one of the weasels.

The weasel glared at the Prince and said, "You there! You're under arrest." But before he could grab the Prince, a peasant threw a tomato at the weasel's pointy little face.

"Run for it!" the peasant cried to the Prince.

But the Prince didn't run away. Instead he grabbed a leg of ham. Using the ham leg as a sword, he started a full-fledged duel with the guards. The crowd watched excitedly as the Prince jabbed at a weasel. Then the Prince ducked up and down to dodge the weasel's iron sword.

The weasel was getting in a few jabs of his own. Slices of meat were flying everywhere! The weasel was using his sword to slice them off of the Prince's leg of ham!

"Gawrsh! Hang on, Mickey, I'm coming," Goofy shouted from the back of the crowd.

Goofy rushed to his friend's aid. He jumped on a barrel and rolled toward the wagon. The barrel hit a rock and Goofy flew into the air. He landed in the wagon, startling the Royal Provisioner's horse. The animal went wild with fear! He stampeded up the street with the wagon clattering behind. Then the runaway wagon plowed through the pack of weasels that was attacking Mickey.

"Whoooooaaa!" Goofy cried.

Goofy grabbed the Prince by the collar and pulled him into the cart, as the weasels were knocked over like bowling pins.

"C'mon, Mickey!" Goofy screamed.

"Thank you, Goofy," the Prince replied.

The wagon raced down the street. Goofy gulped in fear. The wagon was heading toward a brick wall! He tried dragging his big feet on the ground to slow down the wagon. But it was no use.

CRASH! The wagon slammed through the brick wall — carrying Goofy and the Prince to safety!

10

"Now, I may be losing my mind, Captain. I know you've said that over and over again. But all I know is he acted like a nobleman, and he had the royal ring," explained the weasel.

After the battle, the weasels stole back whatever food they could from the crowd. Then they raced to Captain Pete's quarters. Now one of the weasels was giving him a full report of what they had seen in the street.

Captain Pete listened carefully. He took a long puff on his awful-smelling cigar. He flicked his red-hot ashes toward the weasel. "The ring," Captain Pete said thoughtfully. "So it *was* the Prince I booted out."

The weasel looked at Captain Pete in disbelief. He started laughing so hard he choked. “You threw out the Prince,” the weasel laughed. “You’re going to get it. Nyaah, nyaah-nyaah-nyaah — ”

The weasel’s teasing was choked off when Captain Pete grabbed him around the neck. “Not if he doesn’t come back alive,” Captain Pete said slowly. He let go of the weasel’s neck. The gasping weasel dropped to the floor.

The Captain stroked his stubbled chin. He smiled the evil grin he always smiled when he was hatching a plan.

Captain Pete ordered the weasel to bring him the dog that had wandered into the castle with the peasant.

The weasel smiled an evil smile at the Captain. He wasn’t quite sure what Captain Pete had in mind. But whatever it was, it was sure to be bad.

11

At that very moment the peasant himself was in the game room, having a sword fight with an empty suit of armor. Mickey bent his legs low in his best fencing stance. He slashed at the armor with his sword.

"Knave! Villain!" Mickey shouted at his make-believe opponent. "Take that! And that!" Mickey smiled to himself. He was getting to like this prince business.

Mickey's pretend duel was cut short by a knock at the game room door. "Enter," Mickey said in his most princely voice. He spun around to see who dared interrupt his battle.

Mickey turned so quickly that his sword flew out of his hand! The weapon soared across the room. It hit its mark — cutting Horace's hat in two! Horace was very surprised — and relieved. Another inch, and the sword would have skewered poor Horace!

"Oops!" Mickey said, with a very unprincely blush of embarrassment.

"Nice shot, sire," Horace said sarcastically. Then he looked seriously at Mickey.

"Your Highness," Horace said sadly, "your father is in his last hours. He wishes to see you at once."

The King was dying! Mickey was so upset that he forgot he was supposed to be the Prince.

"Oh, uh . . ." he said shakily. "We'd better tell the Prince. He'd want to see him!"

Horace was confused. "You are the Prince, sire," he said.

Mickey kicked nervously at the shiny marble floor with his big toe. "Well, uh . . . I've been meaning to talk to you about that."

Horace grew stern. This was no time for games. "Sire, please," Horace said as he took

Mickey by the arm and started to drag him down the hall. "The King is gravely ill."

As soon as they reached the door to the King's bedroom, Horace turned to leave. Mickey grabbed his sleeve and begged him to stay. Mickey didn't want to be left alone with the dying King, especially since Mickey was not really the King's son.

But Horace shook his head. The schoolteacher did not belong there. This was a time for the King and the Prince to be alone together. Horace choked back a tear, turned, and walked slowly down the hall.

Mickey took a deep breath. There was only one thing to do. "I'll explain everything," Mickey said to himself. "The King will understand."

Bravely, Mickey entered the King's bedroom. The King's chambers were dark. When he looked over at the old man, Mickey's eyes filled with tears. The King was very weak. His eyes were shut and his face was very white.

"My son," the King said in a thin, croaking voice.

“But — ” Mickey began.

“Come closer,” the King interrupted.

Mickey walked over to the bed and took the old man’s bony hand in his. He leaned closer to hear what the King was saying.

“My son,” the King said in a thin, weak voice. “From the day you were born I have tried to prepare you for this moment. I shall be gone soon, and you will be King. You must promise . . . promise me that you will rule the land from your heart, justly and wisely.”

The King’s voice was barely a whisper now. He had very little time left to live. Mickey bowed his head. He knew now that he could not reveal his true identity. Mickey had to let the King die in peace. He squeezed the King’s hand tightly.

“I promise,” Mickey said softly.

With a heavy heart, Mickey left the King’s bedside. He shut the door quietly behind him. Mickey knew that he had to find the Prince and tell him about his father’s death.

“Where is he?” Mickey said as he hurried down the hall.

Suddenly a big, hairy hand reached out

and grabbed Mickey from behind. The hand lifted him off the ground. Mickey turned to see Captain Pete's evil eyes staring at him!

"What the . . . ? Hey! Unhand me!" Mickey shouted. He tried to wriggle free from Captain Pete's grasp.

"Good day, my phony prince," Captain Pete snarled.

"Guards! Seize him!" Mickey ordered. But the weasels didn't make a move. Mickey started to panic. The Prince hadn't told him what to do if saying "Guards! Seize him!" didn't work!

"Shut your mouth!" Captain Pete barked. "Now that our dearly departed King is out of my way, you're going to do exactly what I say. 'Cause if you don't . . ."

Captain Pete moved aside to let Mickey see his other prisoner.

"Pluto!" Mickey cried.

Captain Pete pulled hard on Pluto's leash, and the poor pup let out a yelp of pain.

Captain Pete grinned. "Get the picture?" he asked wickedly.

12

Out on the streets, church bells tolled all over London. The bells always rang when there was important news in the land.

Goofy stood in the kitchen of his little shack, cooking soup for dinner. The Prince sat quietly and nursed the nasty bruises he had gotten in the battle with the weasels. Hearing the bells, the Prince leaned out the window and questioned a passing driver.

"You there," he called. "What happened?"

"The King is dead and the Prince is to be crowned at once," the man replied.

The Prince gasped. A tear rolled down his cheek. "Father," he murmured quietly.

"Your soup is almost ready, Mick. I mean, Your Majesty. Hyuck," Goofy called to him. Then he noticed the tears running down the Prince's face. He wondered what had happened.

"Gone. I . . . I can't believe it," the Prince was saying to himself. The Prince wiped his eyes and stood tall. He pulled the royal ring from his pocket and slipped it on his finger. "Now it is up to me," he said bravely. "I must right the wrongs I have seen. Children going hungry. Corruption everywhere."

Goofy stared at the Prince in amazement. "Gawrsh, you really are the Prince, aren't you?" he said. Goofy bowed so low his long black ears touched the floor. "Sire, your wish is my command."

The Prince placed his hand under Goofy's chin. He gestured for Goofy to rise. "Goofy, I owe you my life," the Prince said. "This will not be forgotten. Come, friend. We must return to the palace at once."

"Or a visit to the dungeon, my Prince!" a deep voice interrupted. Captain Pete burst through the door. Behind him were his faithful weasel guards. "Get 'em, boys!" the Captain ordered. The weasels threw their swords with perfect aim. They landed in the shape of a cage around the Prince. The Prince was Captain Pete's prisoner!

Goofy picked up an old broom and swung it wildly in the air. "On guard!" he called to the weasels from behind his broom sword. He had to protect the Prince!

The weasels fought back by throwing spears at Goofy. Hundreds of spears whizzed past. Goofy ducked up and down and from side to side. He waved his broom handle angrily.

One of the sharp arrows snagged Goofy by the pants. The powerful spear flew toward the window — carrying Goofy with it! The spear stuck in the windowsill, pinning Goofy's baggy pants to the wall. The poor guy slid out of his pants and went soaring headfirst out the window!

"Ya-ha-ha-whooeeee!" Goofy cried on the way down to the sidewalk below.

Captain Pete snatched up the Prince and ran down to the wagon.

He couldn't stop laughing as the wagon made its way back to the castle — and the dungeon!

13

The dungeon was dark and damp. Water leaked from the pipes and dripped down the walls to the floor. Donald sat alone in the cold, smelly darkness, muttering in anger. He couldn't believe that the Captain of the Guards had the nerve to put him in the dungeon. After all, he was the Prince's faithful servant!

All of a sudden, Donald turned around and squawked with fear. Behind him was a white, staring skeleton!

"Wak!" Donald jumped up in fright. "Let me out of here!"

Donald made a run for the door. Then he heard a key jiggling in the lock. Donald almost jumped for joy! Freedom!

But Donald couldn't have been more

wrong. Captain Pete was just sending in another prisoner to keep Donald company. When Donald saw the new prisoner, he couldn't believe his eyes. It was the Prince!

"You'll pay for this, Captain!" the Prince declared as he squirmed in Captain Pete's powerful grasp. "I command you to put me down right now!"

"After the pauper's crowned, it will be good-bye to you!" Captain Pete sneered as he threw the Prince down the narrow, winding dungeon stairs.

The Prince tumbled head over heels down the stairs. He bashed right into Donald, who crashed into the wall.

"Waaak!! Wak!" Donald cried out in pain. Then he sat up and rubbed his eyes. "Your Highness!" Donald said hopefully. "We're saved!" In a split second, Donald's joy turned to fear. "Wait a minute, you're in here, too! We're doomed!"

Toot-doo-doo-too!

In the distance, the Prince could hear the trumpets sounding a royal fanfare.

"The coronation!" the Prince exclaimed

in horror. If he didn't do something very soon the beggar boy would be crowned King of England!

Quickly the Prince scurried up the dungeon stairs to the door. "This has gone on long enough! I demand that you open this door immediately!" he ordered the guard.

"Oh, be quiet," the guard answered through the bars in the cell-door window.

Soon the Prince heard heavy footsteps coming down the hallway toward the dungeon. He looked out in fear as a tall man wearing a black leather hood walked up to the guard. The masked stranger carried a sharp ax on a long handle.

The guard nodded to the hooded man and explained to the Prince, "Looks like the boss isn't wasting any time! Hee, hee, hee . . ." It was the executioner.

The guard stepped aside gleefully. The executioner's job was to cut off the heads of the prisoners. "Be my guest, pal," he said.

The executioner walked toward the dungeon door, balancing his ax on his shoulder. Whoops! The executioner stepped in a bucket of soapy water, and almost chopped off the guard's head with his ax! The guard was lucky that the blade got stuck in the wall behind him instead.

"Hey! What's the big idea?!" the guard whined.

"Hyuck! Sorry," the executioner apologized as he tried to pry the ax out of the wall.

Harder and harder the executioner pulled, until finally, his ax came loose — and smashed the guard on the back of the head!

"Thank you, I've had a lovely evening," the guard mumbled foolishly as he tumbled to the ground.

The executioner removed his hood. He looked down at the fallen guard. "Gawrsh" was all he said.

The Prince studied the executioner's long ears, buck teeth, and large clumsy hands. That was no executioner. That was Goofy!

"Just sit tight, little buddy!" Goofy said. "I'll have you out of there in a jiffy!"

Toot-doo-doo-too. The horns sounded again. *Hurry, Goofy, hurry,* the Prince thought.

14

Goofy took a ring of keys from the pocket of the unconscious guard. "Now let me see here," he said as he fiddled with the keys. "Was it the skinny one? The round one with the fat end?" One by one, Goofy studied the keys. "Maybe it was this little one."

As Goofy examined every single key on the key ring, the weasel guard woke up. Goofy was too busy to notice. Swiftly the guard stuck two fingers in his mouth and whistled. Immediately, other weasels appeared as if out of nowhere.

The Prince tried desperately to warn Goofy that a whole pack of weasel guards was right behind him. But Goofy wouldn't turn around. He was still trying to figure out which key would open the lock. "Maybe it was the gold one. Nope, that's not it. Maybe this great big one . . ."

Donald couldn't wait any longer. He reached through the bars. He grabbed the key ring from Goofy's hands. The cranky valet slammed one key into the lock and turned the key.

The door flew open. The Prince and Donald raced out the door into the long, dark tunnel that connected the dungeon to the palace. Goofy followed close behind.

The weasel guards were right on their tails. One of them was waving a long, pointed dagger. The dagger was so close to Goofy he could feel it.

"Wow! That thing's sharp!" Goofy yelped.

Finally the Prince reached a door and opened it. He looked out, then down. They were high above ground! The door led nowhere!

One of the weasels threw his dagger at Goofy. The knife missed Goofy, but it snagged Goofy's pants and stuck in the door.

The Prince thought fast. He flung the

door open wide. Then he, Donald, and Goofy held tight to the handle of the dagger. As the Prince's feet dangled in the air, the weasel guards ran past him — out the door, and straight down to the ground.

"Eeeeeyaaaaa!" they squealed as they fell.

15

In the Great Hall, members of the royal court had gathered to watch the Prince be crowned the King of England. They had no idea that at that very minute the real Prince was escaping from the clutches of the weasels. They did not know that the fellow in the hallway was not a prince, but a pauper.

Mickey stood outside the Great Hall dressed in a thick red velvet cape. It was time for the Prince to be crowned. Horace walked down the hallway in front of Mickey, leading the way to the Great Hall.

Mickey wanted to stop Horace. He wanted to tell him they had the wrong one. But every time Mickey opened his mouth,

Captain Pete gave a rough tug on Pluto's leash. Mickey had no choice. He would have to enter the Great Hall.

There was only one thing Mickey could do. He had to stall. Maybe he could hold off the crowning until the real Prince got there.

The Prince had better hurry, Mickey thought nervously to himself. *I can only stall for so long.*

Very slowly, Mickey walked down the long aisle. It seemed to go on forever. Eventually Mickey stepped up to the King's throne. The Archbishop was standing nearby.

"Be seated, sire," the Archbishop said, pointing to the throne.

"No, after you," Mickey said, stalling.

"No, no, sire. Beauty before age," the Archbishop said and smiled.

"Ah . . . no. Age before beauty," Mickey answered.

"Your Highness, you're such a sport," the Archbishop laughed, then said in a stern voice, "Sit down."

Mickey gulped. "Got it," he said. He sat obediently on the throne.

The Archbishop lifted the royal crown. The people *oohed* and *aahed* at its beauty.

"It is both my duty and my pleasure . . . to . . . crown . . ." the Archbishop began. He tried to put the crown on Mickey's head. Mickey kept dodging him. If the Archbishop moved the crown to the left, Mickey moved his head to the right. If the Archbishop moved the crown to the right, Mickey moved his head in the opposite direction.

"It is both my honor and duty to . . . crown you," the Archbishop tried again. "I say, a rather wiry lad," he remarked before adding, "would you hold still!"

Finally, Mickey made one last desperate attempt to stop the ceremony. Mickey took a deep breath. "Stop!" he cried out.

Captain Pete stared at Mickey. He couldn't believe the little pauper would ignore his threats. "What the — " Captain Pete began.

"Look, I'm the Prince, right?" Mickey

said nervously. "And whatever I order must be done, right?"

The Archbishop looked confused. "Uh . . ." he answered.

"Well, then . . . the Captain is a thief! Guards, seize him!" Mickey ordered, pointing to Captain Pete.

Captain Pete's face turned red with anger. "Seize him," he hissed to the guards. Pete pointed to Mickey. "He's an imposter!"

"But *I'm* not, Captain," a loud voice shouted from the windowsill above as the guards surrounded Mickey.

Mickey breathed a heavy sigh of relief. The Prince had arrived just in time!

16

Captain Pete couldn't believe his eyes. The Prince had escaped! The Captain shook with fear. He was in big trouble!

The Prince leaped from the window ledge. The crowd gasped as he grabbed hold of the giant crystal chandelier and swung across the ceiling.

As he moved through the air, the Prince swiped a sword from a guardsman beneath him. "Thank you, guardsman," the Prince said with a royal tip of his hat.

The Prince landed solidly — right at Captain Pete's feet. The Prince smiled slowly. Then he pointed the sharp metal sword at the Captain.

Captain Pete backed nervously away. "Now, now, now, wait a minute, Your Majesty," Captain Pete stuttered as he stepped back. "I can explain everything!"

Ever so slowly, the Prince put his sword down. "Very well, I await your explanation," he said.

Captain Pete bowed very low. As he spoke, he grabbed hold of the carpet beneath the Prince's feet. "Your Majesty is too kind . . ." he began.

"Look out, sire!" Mickey tried to warn the Prince.

But it was too late. Mean old Captain Pete pulled the rug right out from under the Prince.

The Prince was caught off guard. He stumbled. Then he lost his grip on his sword. The crowd gasped. The Prince seemed doomed!

The Captain raised his sword and lunged toward the shaken Prince. But the Prince had recovered his grip. He was a far better fighter than Captain Pete thought. By moving from side to side the Prince was able to fight off Captain Pete's sword.

A weasel guard crept up behind the

Prince. The weasel picked up his bow and arrow and aimed it at the Prince's back!

Goofy and Donald hurried into action. Without thinking, they jumped off the window ledge in hopes of landing on the crystal chandelier. Whoops! The two heroes missed the chandelier and plunged toward the crowd.

"Geronimoooooooo," Goofy cried on the way down.

Plop! Goofy landed in a big heap — on top of the weasel who was about to shoot the Prince. But the weasel fired the arrow anyway.

The arrow soared across the room toward Pluto. It cut through the rope that kept him prisoner. The rope snapped. Pluto was free!

Barking, Pluto jumped into action.

17

The battle raged on in full force. The Prince and his loyal pals fought hard against Captain Pete and the weasels.

Goofy grabbed a bow and arrow. He pulled the arrow back and got ready to shoot. "Hold on, sire," he called. "I'll — !" But he did not finish his sentence. Plunk! Donald backed up and fell on top of him. Goofy never got to shoot his arrow. He was too busy trying to lift Donald off of him.

The poor Prince wasn't doing much better. Captain Pete was holding the Prince at swordpoint.

Captain Pete stared down at the helpless Prince. He licked his lips. The Captain had the Prince right where he wanted him!

The Captain flashed his sword in the air.

Quickly, the Prince ducked. The sword barely missed him.

The Captain swung again. This time his sword came even closer! But it wasn't the Prince who screamed out in pain — it was Captain Pete himself! Pluto had bit him in the behind.

Goofy and Donald wanted to get in on the action. Donald stood behind Goofy, holding a bag of arrows in his hands. Goofy held the bow. He reached behind him and grabbed the biggest arrow he could find. Then he loaded the arrow, pulled back on the bow, and let go. The arrow soared across the room.

Goofy looked up with surprise. That was no arrow! That was Donald! Goofy had shot the Prince's valet across the room instead of the arrow!

The flying valet whooshed high above the heads of the crowd. He smashed billfirst into a tall column and stuck there, vibrating up and down — just like a real arrow.

At the same time, the Prince ran to hide behind the tall throne. Mickey followed him.

Captain Pete saw them and raced to the throne, sword in hand.

First Mickey popped his head out from behind the right side of the throne. Captain Pete swung at Mickey's head. Next the Prince popped his head out from behind the left side of the throne. Captain Pete looked confused. But he aimed his sword at the Prince.

Mickey and the Prince moved back and forth behind the throne. Captain Pete was getting very upset. Which one was the real Prince?

Finally Captain Pete got an idea. He plunged his sword into the middle of the throne. He started to saw the old chair in half.

Mickey ducked out of the way just in time! The chair split in two! Captain Pete smiled with glee. But his smile soon turned to a frown. Where was the Prince?

"Up here, Captain," the Prince called from the top of what was left of the royal throne. As Captain Pete stared up in surprise, the Prince grabbed hold of a banner that hung nearby. With one good yank, the Prince ripped the banner from the wall and dropped it over Captain Pete's head. The cruel Captain's arms waved around him as he struggled to get out from under the heavy banner.

The Prince smiled and picked up his sword. But the Prince wasn't paying attention. A weasel snuck up behind him. He lifted his arms high to clobber the Prince!

Mickey jumped up and bashed the weasel on the head. The weasel swayed for a second. Then he fell slowly to the ground.

"Thanks, Mickey," the Prince said with a quick handshake.

"No problem," Mickey smiled back.

But in a second Mickey discovered he had a lot of problems. And they were all charging straight toward him! On the command "Charge!" a whole gang of weasels dashed in Mickey's direction!

Seeing the running weasels, Goofy yanked at Donald's feet. He tried again and again to pry Donald loose from the column. Goofy pulled with all his might.

One, two, three. Donald popped out of the wall. The force knocked both of them to the ground!

Goofy and Donald went rolling across the floor. Before they knew it, they were rolled up inside a large carpet! The carpet rolled across the floor and didn't stop moving until it smashed into a suit of armor that was leaning against the wall.

The suit of armor rocked back and forth for a second. Then the armor's ax fell. In one swift movement the ax cut the rope that held the giant crystal chandelier.

The glittering chandelier tumbled to the ground. It landed right on top of the weasel army. The weasels were trapped!

Captain Pete stopped fighting just long enough to look at his guards. In that second the Prince lunged at him. He knocked the sword from the Captain's hands. Captain Pete was finished.

With one last thrash of his sword, the Prince sliced through Captain Pete's belt. The Captain's big trousers fell to the floor. The crowd began to howl with laughter.

There stood the evil Captain Pete — wearing little more than a pair of white boxer shorts, with big red hearts drawn all over them! He did not look very scary now!

The crowd laughed even harder.

Captain Pete was very embarrassed. He tried to cover himself. But before he could, the rolling weasel chandelier barreled across the floor at top speed. It ran over the Captain. Before anyone knew it Captain Pete was tied up tight inside the chandelier!

18

"Boy, am I glad to see you!" Mickey said as he gave the Prince a big hug.

"But what a time I've had," the Prince sighed.

The Archbishop was still holding the royal crown. He looked from one lad to the other. Both were small. Both had the same features. Both were wearing clothing torn in battle. The Archbishop could not tell the Prince from the pauper.

"Good heavens! But which one is which?" the Archbishop asked.

Pluto knew the answer. He dashed across the room and leaped into the arms of his beloved master, Mickey.

Pluto licked Mickey's face excitedly. His tail wagged wildly.

"Guess there's no fooling you, boy," Mickey giggled. He hugged Pluto tight.

The Archbishop walked over to the Prince. Gently, he placed the jewel-covered crown on his head. "Therefore I crown you the Prince . . . uh, King of England," the Archbishop announced.

Mickey raised a glass high in the air. "Everybody say a toast to the King," he said with a bow. "Long live the King!"

Epilogue

And so, the young King set out to right the wrongs of his country. To do so, the King asked the help of his new friends. Because of his bravery, the King named Goofy the Captain of the Guards. And because of his generosity, the King named Mickey the Royal Provisioner.

The King never forgot the lessons he learned when he and Mickey had traded places. For the rest of his days, he ruled his kingdom with fairness and compassion.